JACOB
of the
Little People

~ A Christmas Tale ~

prose and paintings by
JAMES M. ELLINGSWORTH

ISBN: 1456543237
ISBN-13: 9781456543235

to my daughter emma, and alyssa, who taught me to hold close and always value the child inside of me

To Michael and Hannah,

Merry Christmas!

J. Giurgounte

Everyone knows the stories about Santa and his reindeer, the elves, and the workshop at the North Pole. But the story that few people know is that of the Little People of the North and the work they do during Christmas.

The Little People live in the forest called Enderberry, very near Santa's workshop. Although they resemble elves in appearance, they are smaller in-size, only about six inches tall. They live in tiny houses they carve into the trees. And in the evening, the many shops of Enderberry and the little lanes that line the forest floor are very busy. They live in great harmony with each other, the forest animals, and the trees, and they believe that Christmas is the most cherished time of the year.

Because they are so small and no one ever sees them, the Little People's story is seldom told. But Santa knows how important their job is during Christmas, and he holds the Little People in very high regard.

Every year, a few weeks before Christmas, Santa holds a meeting with the Little People in the Great Hall. At this meeting Santa goes through a long list of names, places and addresses, assigning one to each of the Little People. The Little People would then travel to their assigned home, where it would be their job to make sure that the family who lived there had the best Christmas ever.

Aside from Christmas Eve, this is the biggest night of the year for the Little People. They all arrive for the meeting dressed in their Christmas uniforms. And this particular year, no one was more excited than Jacob.

Jacob was slightly smaller than the rest of the Little People, and with his fuzzy beard and red curly hair, he stood out from the others. He was shy but determined, scared but brave. This was his first time leaving the North Pole, and he was excited to be able to finally prove himself to Santa.

After Santa had given his final speech about the Christmas spirit, the meeting ended. Santa made his way through the crowd, stopping Jacob before he left. He gently picked Jacob up and smiled at him.

"So, Jacob, this is your first time leaving the North Pole. Are you ready?"

"Yes, Santa, I am. I will be leaving soon."

"Well, I have given you a very special family this year, and they will need your help more than ever this Christmas season."

"Thank you, Santa, I will do my best."

Santa nodded. "Very good Jacob, I will see you again on Christmas Eve."

The day Jacob was ready to leave, a large bird called, a whip-poor-will, arrived to take him to his new home. The sleek bird crouched down and, Jacob tied a large sack to its leg. Everything he needed was in the sack. Jacob climbed onto the bird's back, and with a beautiful song, the whip-poor-will took flight. They had a long journey ahead of them.

The bird flew for three days and nights, through storms and strong winds. On the last day of the journey, after flying all night, Jacob saw the sun rising over the mountains as he arrived at a small yellow house. The house sat upon a mountain surrounded by trees. It had a large front porch with a white picket fence around the yard. It was a beautiful little house, and he immediately felt at home.

Jacob untied the sack, petted the birds beak and thanked it, and the bird flew away.

Jacob began looking for the right tree for his new home. He walked for a bit, inspecting each tree carefully, until he came upon a very nice oak in the front yard of the house.

"This will be my new home," he said.

He pulled his trusty axe from the sack and began chopping away at the base of the tree. He began to carve, and in no time, his new home was ready.

Christmas was coming. It snowed that first night and Jacob spent his days gathering firewood and making his house cozy.

The late-autumn days were cool and the nights were chilly. Soon the Christmas tree and the decorations would go up, and Jacob could begin his work.

One day Jacob saw a woman and a little girl bring all the Christmas decorations out and begin to put them up. They hung the outside lights, and Jacob watched through the window as they hung the stockings on the mantel and put Christmas candles all about the living room. Then they went for a drive. When they came back, they had a huge Christmas tree tied to the roof of their car. They put it up in the front window and decorated it with balls and lights, popcorn strings and pine cones. It was a beautiful tree.

That night, Jacob wrapped himself in a blanket and made his way into the house. This time it was magical. He felt a glow in his heart as he admired the Christmas tree, and all the decorations. Although Jacob had always understood the spirit of Christmas, it wasn't until this very moment that he finally knew what Santa meant and what his work was all about.

Jacob did his best to keep the Christmas spirit going for the family in the little house. He fixed the outside lights when they came off the gutters, and he made sure the Christmas wreaths on the doors and windows were full. Then he would go inside and climb the tree, making sure all the lights worked and he would shine all the Christmas balls. He checked that everything had fresh batteries and was plugged in and working. He enjoyed his work very much.

Before the family got home, Jacob would turn on all the Christmas lights, inside and out, and then listened as the little girl gleefully shouted that Santa must be coming, for who else could have done this Christmas magic? Jacob was doing his job well and felt certain that Santa would be pleased.

One night when he was in the house, Jacob noticed a burned-out light bulb on the Christmas tree. He carefully climbed up, unscrewed the bulb, and replaced it with a new one. But the sudden brightness of the new bulb startled him, and he accidentally dropped the old one! He gasped as it hit the floor with a loud 'POP'! He lost his balance, falling over backwards he somehow got his leg tangled in the light cord. Terrified, Jacob hung upside down with the cord wrapped around his leg, swinging back and forth.

Suddenly the upstairs light came on, and he heard the little girl coming down the steps. She made her way to the tree and looked down at the broken glass. Then she looked up and saw Jacob dangling in the air. He tried to stay very still. She moved towards him and smiled.

"Hello, my name is Emma. Do you need some help?" she asked.

Jacob did not know what to do. Little People were never supposed to be seen or even known about. But Emma looked friendly, and he was stuck.

"Yes, please, I suppose I could use some help getting down from here."

Emma gently un-wrapped the cord from his leg and held him carefully in her hand. Jacob stood frozen in the palm of her hand, staring into her big blue eyes.

"Who are you?" she asked.

Jacob began to relax. He could tell that Emma was a very special girl. They sat beneath the tree and he told her about the Little People, and how Santa had sent him to help her family during Christmas. Somehow he knew she would keep his secret.

She listened and smiled at Jacob's story. Then her eyelids grew heavy and she yawned.

"You'd better get off to bed," Jacob said.

"Yes, I am very tired."

"Good night, Emma. I'll see you again soon."

"Good night, Jacob," said Emma as she made her way up the stairs.

Over the next couple of weeks, Emma and Jacob became very close. They played each day in the snow, riding Emma's sled, building snowmen, waiting and wishing for Christmas. At night Jacob went into the house and made sure all was well.

He was right on schedule for Christmas and everything was going fine. Then one day, as Emma and Jacob were walking through the snow Jacob asked,

"What do you want for Christmas Emma?"

She stopped and looked down at her boots. "All I want for Christmas is for my daddy to come home. Mommy said he had to go away but that he should be home for Christmas."

Could Santa possibly give her this gift? , Jacob wondered. So Jacob was determined to work even harder to make Emma's Christmas special.

Finally, Christmas eve arrived, snowing and windy. Jacob spent the day preparing for Santa and getting his Christmas uniform ready. He built a fire at his home and made himself a cup of hot cocoa. In the house, Emma and her mother were baking cookies and wrapping presents.

As the day went on, the weather turned colder and the snow fell harder. By nightfall, all the Christmas lights were on and the tree was shining. Now all Jacob had to do was wait for Santa. Finally he saw most of the lights go out inside the house, and he changed into his Christmas uniform.

Jacob pulled on his hat, gloves and coat, and made his way to the house. He had a hard time making his way through the deep snow. Once inside he saw that Emma and her mother had put out chocolate chip cookies and a tall glass of milk for Santa. They had lit Christmas candles, and the fireplace was now only glowing embers. The house was warm and cozy, and Jacob climbed up to the mantle to wait.

As Jacob sat, he watched the snow fall outside. He started to doze off, tired from all the excitement. Suddenly, there was a very loud "SNAP" from outside, and then all the Christmas lights flickered and went out!

Looking out the window, he saw that a large tree branch, heavy from snow and blown by the wind, had fallen on the electrical wires. The branch lay on the wires cutting off the power to the house. Putting his hat, gloves and coat on again, he rushed outside, wondering how he could possibly fix this!

He fought his way through the deep snow to his home. He got the longest rope he could find and his trusty axe. He scrambled up the tree toward the broken branch.

He tied one end of the rope around his waist and the other around the power line.

He swung himself towards the branches and chopped away each time he came near it.

He chopped away one part of the broken branch, then another, and then one more. Now only one small branch lay on the power line.

The branch was small but stubborn. He chopped and chopped, until at last it fell away. He dangled dangerously from the line for a moment. Then suddenly all the Christmas lights outside and inside the house turned back on! Jacob climbed back down and made his way back to the house, and not a moment too soon.

As Jacob sat breathless on the mantel, he heard the clatter of Santa's sleigh on the roof. He heard sounds coming from the chimney, and then Santa making his way down.

Santa stood up, put down his bag, and brushed the ashes from his shoulders. He turned and looked up at Jacob.

"Hello, Jacob, merry Christmas!, How are you, my little friend?"

Jacob stood and smiled in his neatly pressed Christmas uniform.

"All….is well…. Santa," he managed to say.

"It's a nasty night out. Thank you for keeping all the lights on. Are you alright?"

"Yes, Santa," replied Jacob.

"Good. Well then, can you please fill the stockings while I put all the presents out?"

They worked together, Jacob filling the stockings with Christmas goodies while Santa placed the presents around the tree. Finally they were done, and Santa sat down to eat his cookies and drink his milk.

"You've done well, Jacob. The house is warm and full of Christmas spirit. Everything is perfect."

"Thank you, Santa."

Santa grabbed his empty bag and moved towards the chimney. "I must be off. I will see you back at the North Pole."

"Santa," said Jacob. " The little girl, Emma, she really only wants one thing for Christmas."

"This I know, Jacob. You must believe in the spirit of Christmas. Sometimes miracles do happen…"

"Goodbye Santa," said Jacob

"Goodbye, my small friend." Santa said. And placing his finger on his nose, he shot up the chimney.

Jacob sat for a moment and looked around. The house was glowing, and finally he felt proud about what he had done. He decided to look in on Emma before he left. Slowly he made his way up to her room.

She was asleep, a slight smile on her face. Jacob hoped this would be her best Christmas ever. With the sun peeking over the trees, Jacob made his way down the steps.

Suddenly the front door opened. There stood a man in a uniform, a duffel bag over his shoulder. He wore heavy boots and a hat. Jacob did not know what to do, so he ran beneath the tree and hid. The man looked around and then opened his bag and placed some presents beneath the tree.

Then Jacob heard Emma from upstairs.

"Daddy?"

"Emma? Is that you?" Tears glistened in the man's eyes. "Merry Christmas sweetie..."

Emma ran downstairs and jumped into the man's arms, and he held her close. Her father had come home.

Jacob returned to his home and slept most of Christmas day. He was very tired. In the evening he peered through the front window one last time. The tree glowed and all the presents had been opened. The candles flickered and a warm fire burned in the fireplace. Emma, her father, and her mother were laughing and enjoying Christmas dinner. Jacob had never felt happier.

Emma really had the best Christmas ever.

Jacob packed his things. A few days after Christmas, he was ready to go. He was sad to be leaving but happy to be going home. The sky was blue, and the sun reflected brightly off the snow.

Just then, Emma came out of the house and walked over to Jacob.

"Are you leaving now?" she asked.

"Yes, Emma, I need to get back to the North Pole."

"Here, I made something for you." She handed him a small gift wrapped in shiny paper. He opened it carefully. Inside was a bracelet made of many different colored strings.

"Oh, Emma, it's beautiful!" he said.

"It's a friendship bracelet. Here, let me help you." She gently placed the bracelet over his shoulder. It made a perfect sash.

"Thank you so much, Emma." She picked him up and hugged him gently.

"Oh, look! Here's my ride." She carefully put him down.

The whip-poor-will landed next to them. Jacob tied his sack to its leg and climbed up.

"Jacob, this has been the best Christmas ever, thank you. I will always think of you!, goodbye!"

"Goodbye Emma, merry Christmas!" Jacob said.

Jacob waved back at Emma. He had a long journey ahead of him, but inside he felt content and happy. He adjusted his sash proudly as the bird took flight and together they soared off into the sky.